Care Bears™

Hugs and Kisses!

GiANT
Coloring and
Activity Book

Modern Publishing
A Division of Unisystems, Inc.
New York, New York 10022
Printed in the U.S.A.
Series UPC: 49565

P9-CRE-162

Welcome to Care-a-lot!

It's fun to share!

1. SWEET DREAMS

One of these pictures of Bedtime Bear is different from the rest. Circle it!

See Answers

Will you be my friend?

Up, Up and Away!

Daydream Bear loves to daydream in the clouds!

Love is what makes the world go 'round!

L O C E V R

_ _ _ _ _ _

2. LUCKY CHARM
Unscramble the letters to see the word for
Good Luck Bear's tummy symbol!

See Answers

Let the sun shine in!

Let's play ball!

Rain, rain, go away!

3. WHAT'S WRONG WITH CHEER BEAR?

Where is Cheer Bear's tummy symbol? Draw one for her! (Hint: It's a rainbow!)

See Answers

I have a secret!

Ice cream always makes Grumpy Bear smile!

Reading is fun!

Best Friends!

4. SO BRIGHT!

Connect the dots from 1 to 15 to see something bright that shines in the sky!

See Answers

Happy Birthday, Champ Bear!

Do you want to play with me?

Get some giggles going!

5. DRAW A CARE BEAR
Draw your favorite Care Bear into the frame.

You feel your best when you do your best!

Reach for the Stars!

Will you read me a bedtime story?

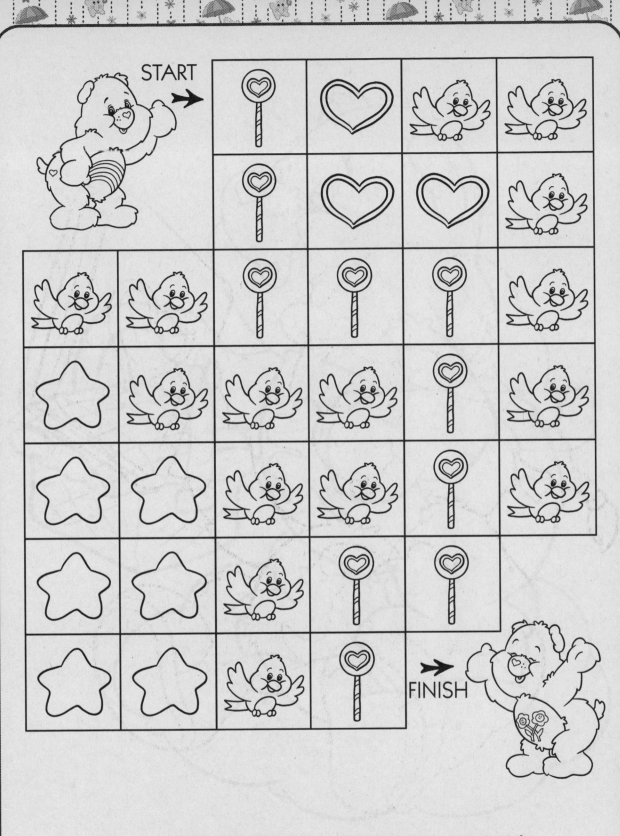

START

FINISH

6. FOLLOW THE LOLLIPOP TRAIL!

Follow the trail made up of lollipops only to help Cheer Bear get to Friend Bear!

See Answers

Let's have a picnic!

Let your happiness glow!

Special Delivery!

7. FUN WITH LETTERS!

Circle the pictures whose names begin with the letter "B"!

See Answers

Tenderheart Bear loves to ride his skateboard!

These cookies are baked with love!

What a pretty butterfly!

_____

8. PRETTY PETALS!

How many petals does the flower have? Write the number on the line.

See Answers

A Day in the Park

Do-Your-Best Bear loves to blow bubbles!

9. PIE IN THE SKY

True Heart Bear wants to bake a pie for the Care Bears. Circle the ingredients that she will need.

See Answers

Daydream Bear and Champ Bear love to play catch!

1=Turquoise 4=Red
2=Yellow 5=Green
3=Blue 6=Orange

10. A PRETTY RAINBOW
Using the color code, color the picture!

Friends Forever!

Flying High!

11. WISHING ON A STAR

Can you help Wish Bear count the stars in the sky?
Write the number of stars that you count on the line.

See Answers

Here's a flower for you, Grumpy Bear!

Care-a-Lot Castle

Sweet dreams, Bedtime Bear!

12. TWO OF HEARTS
Connect each set of dots from 1 to 10 to see
Love-a-lot Bear's tummy symbol!

See Answers

Have I got a friend for you—me!

The secret to friendship is trust!

Today's my lucky day!

Bat
Ball
Mitt

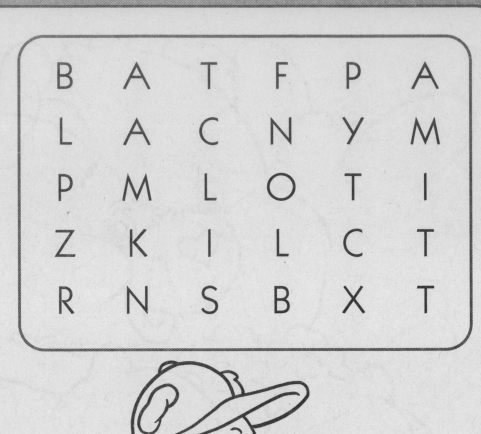

B	A	T	F	P	A
L	A	C	N	Y	M
P	M	L	O	T	I
Z	K	I	L	C	T
R	R	N	S	B	X
					T

13. SPORTY SEARCH

Champ Care Bear is off to his baseball game! Find the words from the word list that describe him in the letter grid. Look up, down, across and diagonally.

See Answers

I love presents!

Sharing is what friends do!

Let's hear it for the Care Bears!

START

FINISH

14. IT'S A SECRET!

Help Secret Bear get through the maze to
Bashful Heart Bear. She has a secret to tell him!

See Answers

15. FUN IN THE SUN IN CARE-A-LOT

Look at the pictures. Circle the items that you can find on a sunny day in Care-a-Lot!

See Answers

Having Fun in the Garden

16. HAPPY BIRTHDAY, CHEER BEAR!
Today is Cheer Bear's birthday! In the space
above, design a special birthday cake for her!

To: _____
From: _____

Will you be my valentine?

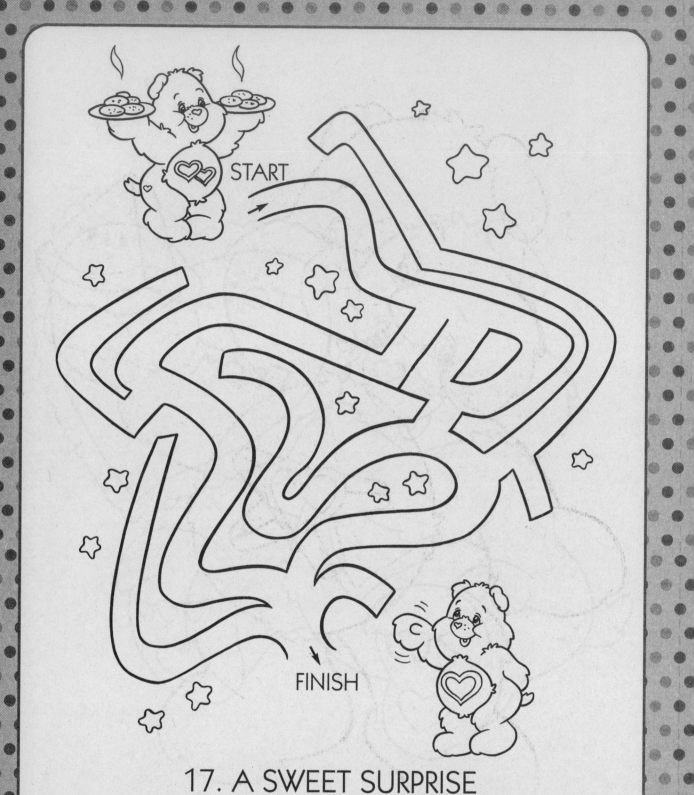

START

FINISH

17. A SWEET SURPRISE

Love-a-lot Bear baked cookies for Tenderheart Bear's birthday! Help Love-a-lot Bear bring the cookies to Tenderheart Bear by finding the correct path through the maze.

See Answers

Time for a Snack!

1.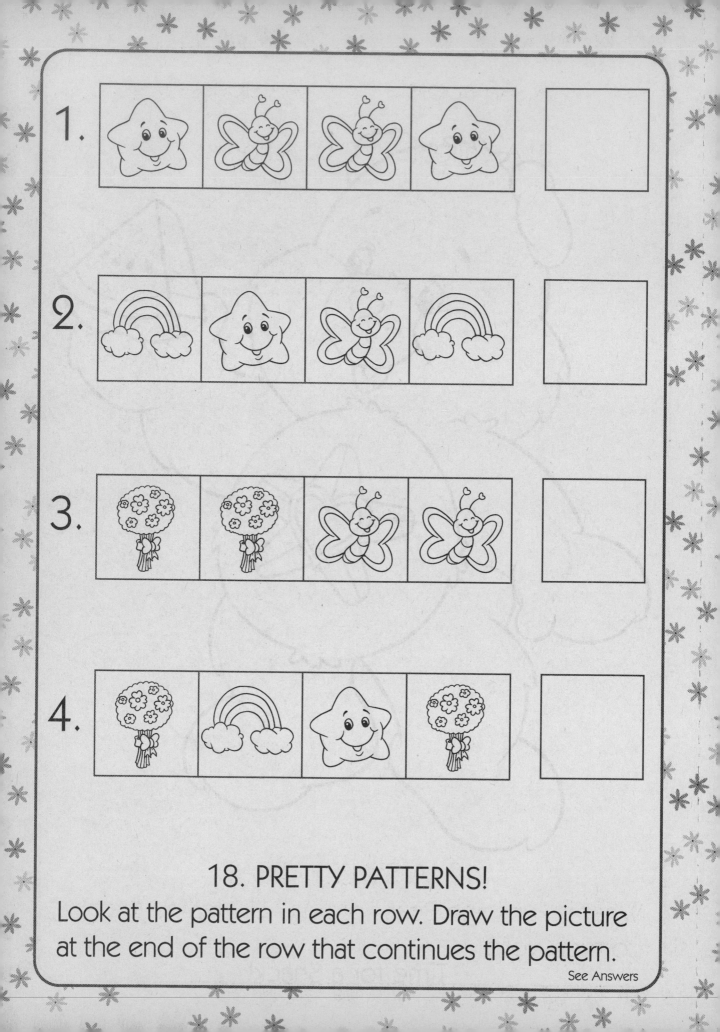

2.

3.

4.

18. PRETTY PATTERNS!
Look at the pattern in each row. Draw the picture
at the end of the row that continues the pattern.

See Answers

A. An apple   C. A cupcake

B. A balloon   D. A flower

19. A SWEET TREAT
What is Funshine Bear holding? Underline the correct word.

What a Great Day!

Going for a Bike Ride

20. A FUNNY FACE!
Circle the Care Bear that is sticking his tongue out!

See Answers

21. HIDE AND SEEK!

Can you find the hidden flower in this picture?
Circle it!

See Answers

E A R C a T L O

_ _ _ _ _ _ - - _ _ _ _

S T A C L E

_ _ _ _ _ _ _

22. HOME SWEET HOME
Unscramble the letters and write them on the lines to find out where the Care Bears love to play!

See Answers

Good Morning!

Sail Away!

23. A RAINY DAY
Draw an object that will protect Grumpy Bear from the rain!

Go Fish!

24. DOUBLE THE FUN!
Which two pictures of Good Luck Bear match?
Circle the identical pair!

See Answers

Hello!

25. FUN WITH SHARE BEAR!

Look at the picture of Share Bear's tummy symbol in the square above. Draw it on Share Bear's tummy!

Love makes a garden grow!

sun

hug

star

run

26. JOIN IN THE FUN!
What words rhyme with the word "fun"? Circle
the balloons that contain the rhyming words!

See Answers

What a Beautiful Day!

Painting the Day Away!

Let's go on a hike!

27. RISE AND SHINE!

Circle the item that will wake Bedtime Bear up in the morning!

See Answers

28. BATTER UP!

Circle the object that Champ Bear will need to hit the ball!

See Answers

Playtime!

See Answers

29. AND THE WINNER IS . . .
What is Tenderheart Bear handing to Champ
Bear? Write the word on the line!

The Care Bears love to share!

30. COUNT THEM UP!

Look at the groups above. Circle the group that shows five. Draw a heart around the group that shows three. Draw a triangle around the group that has two.

See Answers

ANSWERS

1.

3.

2.

C L O V E R

4.

ANSWERS

6.
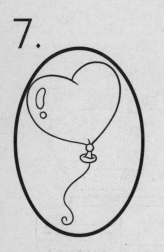

8.

5

7.

9.

ANSWERS

11.

6

13.

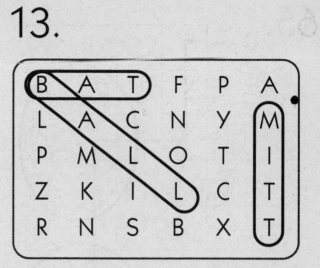

B	A	T	F	P	A
L	A	C	N	Y	M
P	M	L	O	T	I
Z	K	I	L	C	T
R	N	S	B	X	T

12.

14.

START

FINISH

ANSWERS

15.

18.

1.

2.

3.

4.

17.

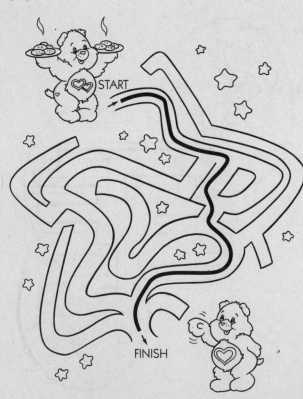

19.

A. An apple   C. A cupcake

B. A balloon   D. A flower

ANSWERS

20.

22.

C A R E - a - L O T

C A S T L E

21.

24.

ANSWERS

26.
sun hug star run

27.

28.

29.

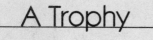
A Trophy

30.